To

CW01086257

Sir ~

From,
David Rogers

ISBN 978-1-4092-4336-6

Published by Lulu.com

The characters in this book are entirely fictional and no resemblance to any real life individuals is stated or implied.

This book is dedicated to India, Erin, Ross, Lauren and Alastair.

Thank you to my wonderful wife, Sarah, for her loving support (and her excellent, free, proof-reading service!).

# The Crystals of Astradan
## ~ *A Lucy McTavish adventure* ~

# 1

"It's my Birthday tomorrow!" shouted Michaela in her usual annoyingly loud voice. "and I'm having a party tonight. The most amazing party anyone has ever had!".

Michaela stood at the bus stop with Jade, Carly and Caitlan. They stood, huddled close together with their backs toward Lucy, who stood by herself a few feet away.

"Would you like to come Jade?", Michaela pointed to Jade as she asked the question.

"Duh….YES!", Jade replied.

"Would you like to come, Carly?".

"I wouldn't miss it for the world kitten!".

Michaela's finger now pointed to the third of her friends.

"And what about you Caitlan?".

"Of course, I'll be where the other kittens are!".

Michaela's face beamed, "Cool! All of the kittens covered then!".

Carly leaned forward towards Michaela's ear as if to whisper to her but in fact her voice was loud enough for all at the bus stop to hear;

"Aren't you going to invite Lucy? I thought you said you were inviting all the girls in class?".

Michaela tilted her head back and looked down her nose towards Lucy.

"No, I said I was inviting all of the *cool* girls in class".

Lucy turned away from the girls and looked at her watch. *The bus should be here in five minutes*, she thought to herself.

Lucy's friends Sally and Zara would be on the bus.

## 2

"Mum, I don't know why those girls are so nasty to me. I've not done anything to them?".

Lucy sat on the sofa with her Mum, who gave her a tight hug.

"Those girls are mean Lucy, don't take any notice of them. You just stick together with Sally and Zara" said Lucy's Mum, reassuring her.

Lucy reached out her arms and hugged her Mum once more. "Love you Mum, Good Night".

"Good Night Lucy, sleep tight, watch the bugs don't bite!".

Lucy popped into the kitchen and picked up her new library book from the bench, putting it under her arm, then picking up the glass of milk from the table.

She walked up the stairs to her bedroom. As she passed Gregor's room she popped her head around the door, which was already open. There was no sign of Gregor. Lucy shouted back downstairs

"Mum, where's Gregor?".

"He's staying out at Josh's house tonight. You've got some peace and quiet!" answered Lucy's Mum.

"Ok Mum, good night".

"Night night sweetheart. No TV mind, it's late".

Lucy closed her bedroom door behind her. She yawned and rubbed her eyes. Tomorrow she was going bowling with Sally and Zara and she couldn't wait. *I hope I get a strike again!* She thought to herself, excitedly.

Lucy got into bed. She thought about reading some of her new library book from school but decided she would save it for later in the weekend. She finished the last of her milk and turned off her bedside lamp. As she lay, she thought about bowling and imagined getting five strikes in a row. She became sleepy and soon her thoughts drifted away from bowling as she fell into a deep, cozy sleep.

# 3

WAKEY WAKEY!

Lucy jumped up in her bed, startled by the strange, metallic voice. She looked around her bedroom, only, it wasn't her bedroom. There were no walls as you'd find in a normal house. Instead the roof of the room was a huge round dome that ran all the way down to the floor. The room was decorated in red paint, with large white dots splattered all around it.

It was no longer dark outside and sunlight beamed through the silver coloured curtains that hung over the small window.

Lucy recognized this room! It was the guest bedroom in Miranda Moon's house in Astradan.

Another noise startled Lucy; this time a loud knock on the bedroom door. WAKEY WAKEY, MISS LUCY!

Lucy jumped from the bed and opened the door. A box-like robot which resembled an old television on legs stood in front of Lucy. It's large eyes were like saucers stuck on it's front.

"Miss Lucy, you are still in your pyjamas! We're going to be late! The Wizard warned that no-one should be late today!". The robot's voice was a little quieter now but just as excited.

"Hello Wembot! Late for what?", Lucy rubbed her eyes to try to wake up a little more.

A small door opened in the side of Wembot and a cable-like arm came out of it, with a metal clasp for a hand on the end. The clasp held a small piece of paper in it's grip, which Lucy took from Wembot.

Lucy read the words that were written on the piece of paper, hoping to find out what Wembot was so excited about:-

*Saturday, 8<sup>th</sup> December*

*A display of magic by Mowban, the 6<sup>th</sup> Wizard of Astradan, in honour of the King and Queen.*
*~ Tulip Green, 8am prompt ~*

"Come Lucy, get dressed and let's hurry or we'll be late!" Wembot began to jump on his short, thick spring-like legs with excitement.

"Ok, give me five minutes Wembot and I'll be right out".

Lucy closed the door and glanced around the room. In a corner there was a chair with some clothes on it and a note from Miranda Moon which read;

*Lucy, I had to leave early today so make yourself comfortable. Here are some clean clothes and make sure you get some breakfast!*

*Oh, and Wembot will be calling for you at 8am to go to the Wizard's show at Tulip Green!*

"No time for breakfast just yet!" Lucy said out loud.

She put on the clothes and ran outside.

"Come on Wembot, let's go!". Lucy ran off down the path as Wembot tried his best to keep up with her, his short legs having to move twice as fast as Lucy's to keep pace.

# 4

The sky was it's usual pink colour. In Astradan, the sky was the brightest shade of pink through the day, and a dark deep purple at night.

As they got to Tulip Green, everyone from the village was there.

"Hi Lucy!" shouted Dillon Batumi, a dark haired, brown-skinned boy who was about the same age as Lucy.

"I saw Miranda earlier, she was helping the Wizard prepare. She said she'll see you shortly after the show".

"Oh that's good" said Lucy smiling and looking around the Green. There must have been one hundred people gathered on Tulip Green.

"Look!", shouted Barney Bracemaine, the baker of Astradan.

"Here come King Boris and Queen Marrilla!".

Lucy looked to her left and saw the King and Queen of Astradan in a wonderful golden chariot, pulled by two beautiful, strong, grey horses.

The chariot pulled up next to Tulip Green and stopped. Bernardo, the King's butler, opened the small door of the open-top chariot and lowered a ramp down to the Green.

The King, a short round man, was dressed in a golden coloured robe with a thousand diamonds stitched into it. He held the Queen's hand as she stepped on to the ramp.

"What a wonderful day for some magic!" shouted the Queen, who was dressed in a gown that was so pure white, Lucy had to look away after a few seconds, for fear it would hurt her eyes.

Everyone on the Green shouted out HURRAY! And gave the Queen a rapturous applause.

As the King was helped down the small ramp from his chariot, by Berndardo, he suddenly lost his footing and slipped.

He fell forward, head first and did a complete forward roll before landing perfectly on his feet, raising his hands in the air, as if commanding an applause.

The crowd on the Green cheered wildly, as the King took a bow.

# 5

Suddenly, the noise from one hundred people gathered on Tulip Green, fell to complete silence as the sound of the banging of a deep drum started to come from the bandstand, in the middle of the Green.

The bandstand was covered by large multi-coloured drapes, so that no-one could see what was in store from the Wizard's magic show.

As the deep-pitched drum continued to pound into the morning sky of Astradan, suddenly, all of the drapes that had surrounded the bandstand fell down to the ground, revealing two tall, strong, bare chested men with huge round drums which stood on the bandstand floor in front of them.

As they pounded out their rhythms, Mowban, the 6th Wizard of Astradan, stood in the middle of them, in the centre of the bandstand.

Dressed in a robe that was as pure white as the queen's dress, and wearing a white hat that must have been as tall as Lucy was, the Wizard raised his hands out to his sides, cast them over his head, then swung his arms down to meet in front of his stomach, his hands making a loud clap.

Everyone on Tulip Green gasped in shock. The drumming stopped and the Wizard spoke, with a powerful, deep voice;

"I, Mowban the 6$^{th}$ Wizard of Astradan, do hereby commence my show of magic, in honour of the King and Queen of the Kingdom of Astradan!".

As he finished speaking, he pulled apart his hands and cast them to the sky – two white doves appeared from his hands and flew into the bright pink sky.

The crowd cheered and clapped excitedly.

The King, who sat with his wife upon two makeshift wooden thrones in the middle of Tulip Green shouted out "Hoorah, hoorah, let us see more, Mowban!".

Next, the two drummers walked to the middle of the bandstand next to Mowban. One kneeled on the floor as the other stood upon his back, protruding one of his arms out forward, towards the wizard.

Mowban produced a wand from his robe and cast it upon the men. There was a bright flash of light and suddenly, in place of the two drummers, stood a magnificent elephant, which rose up onto it's hind legs!

The crowd roared with delight at the wonderful sight before them.

"Wow, the Wizard is really magical!" said Dillon Batumi to Lucy, having to shout, so his voice could be heard above all the noise and excitement.

"And now……" bellowed Mowban.

"….the secret of the magic, of the Wizard's of Astradan".

Mowban produced a small bag from a pocket in his robe. He loosened the drawstrings and emptied the contents into his hand; five small Crystals of amazing, intense colours sat upon his hand, sparkling in the pink daylight.

"Amanna Dabarra, sen durante!", yelled the Wizard and as he did, five rays of amazing bright light shot from the Crystals and flew into the sky. The crowd roared as the lights reigned down upon and amongst them.

As the rays of light finally ceased, the Wizard placed the Crystals back into the bag and tightened the drawstrings.

# 6

"My friends, before I entertain you further, let us not forget that these ancient Crystals, given to us almost one hundred years ago, by the Ancient Knights of Astradan, are what protects and nourishes our kingdom. They are the source of light and warmth in our skies!".

The crowd cheered, clapped and waved their hands energetically. Mowban held the bag of Crystals tightly in his hand and raised his arm towards the sky. The Crystals glowed through the black, suede pouch, as if acknowledging the applause from the crowd.

At that moment, Lucy noticed a large black crow flying through the sky above Tulip Green. It seemed to catch her eye before anyone else's, as it flew across the Green towards the Bandstand.

In a split second, the crow flew right over Mowban's head, plucked the pouch of Crystals from his hand and flew off into the sky.

# 7

The Wizard let out an enormous gasp, and everyone on the Green held their breath in shock.

"No!", shouted Mowban. "Stop that bird, it has the Crystals!".

But there was nothing anyone could do. The crow flew off towards the hills of Sirossa, flying higher and higher each second.

Mowban fell to his knees. "How could I be such a fool!" he asked himself.

"It is not your fault, Mowban" said the King.

"That's right" said Barney Bracemaine. "The Crystals have been in the village for a hundred years. They've never been locked away, yet nothing like this has ever happened. You weren't to know Mowban".

"Mowban, what will happen?", asked the Queen. Her voice was calm but clearly conveyed her worry.

"If the crow flies outside the borders of Astradan, darkness will fall on our kingdom". The Wizard held his head in his hands. "The Crystals must never leave Astradan! Those were the words of the Knights".

"Then we must follow the crow and stop it from leaving the Kingdom" said Elder Corb, the village grocery store owner.

"I fear it is too late for that now", said the King, pointing into the distance – the crow was already some miles away from Tulip Green, and almost out of sight.

# 8

One hour had passed since a black crow had plucked the Crystals of Astradan from Mowban the Wizard's hands, and flown off into the pink skies.

The villagers sat around on Tulip Green, wondering what they could do to get the Crystals back. Although they had seen which direction the crow had flown off in, they had lost sight of it now.

"It's hopeless" said Mowban. Unless the crow happens to fly right back here to Tulip Green, I can't think of a way we can get the Crystals back".

A voice was heard from the crowd; "I'd like to try going after the crow, to see if I can find the Crystals".

It was Lucy McTavish.

"It could be dangerous. The crow flew in the direction of Ness Forest. There may be wild animals or who knows what", said the Queen cautiously.

"The girl is the most suitable among us for the journey", said Mowban.

"She is a Dreamscaper".

Lucy looked around Tulip Green, all of the other people were looking at her now, and she felt a little shy and embarrassed.

"Umm, What is a Dreamscaper?", Lucy finally asked.

Dillon Batumi turned to her "You come to us from another world, in your dreams Lucy".

"Oh…..er, I see" said Lucy, unsure of what else to say.

"Some say Dreamscapers are angels, my dear" said a voice from behind Lucy.

She turned around to see Miranda Moon, smiling warmly.

"Miranda!", she ran up to the tall, elegant lady and gave her a big hug.

"Lucy, the Queen is right. It could be dangerous to go towards Ness Forest. Do you really have a hope of finding the crow or the Crystals?", Miranda Moon placed her hand on Lucy's shoulder caringly, as she asked the question.

"I can only try. I mean it's really important that we get the Crystals back isn't it?" Lucy's eyes were deep and worried.

"Yes it is my dear. You are a brave girl Lucy. Whether a Dreamscaper or not, you are a brave girl".

# 9

"I will go with her" shouted Barney Bracemaine. "I know the paths to the forest well".

"And I will go too, I am small but strong. If we were to find the crow in a tree, I should be able to climb it, and take back the Crystals". This voice came from young Dillon Batumi.

"Then we must go now" said Barney. "We must take advantage of the daylight before nightfall catches us out".

Everyone left Tulip Green and walked the short path back to the main square in the village. Miranda prepared a small bag for Lucy, with some food and water for the journey.

Close to midday, Lucy, Barney Bracemaine and Dillon Batumi left the village, heading South-west towards Ness Forest.

# 10

They walked the long and winding path towards Ness Forest. They couldn't yet see the forest but Barney said they were only about one hour from it now.

Lucy's legs were a little tired but her thoughts were about the forest, and what it may contain. As they approached a small hump-back bridge, Dillon suddenly pointed straight ahead and shouted;

"Look, there's somebody sitting next to the bridge!"

Lucy looked ahead and sure enough a small troll-like figure sat on what looked like a deck chair, slightly hunched but apparently asleep.

His deck chair sat just to the left of the entrance to the small bridge.

"Should we try to pass without waking him?" asked Dillon.

"He is a way-keeper. We should wake him before passing" suggested Barney.

Barney was about fifty years old, a short round man (like most male adults in Astradan), with white hair and a white beard. Lucy noticed how he resembled Father Christmas.

Before they could discuss or decide what to do next, the troll jumped from his deck-chair, placed his hand over his brow to block out the still bright pink daylight, and looked over towards Lucy, Barney and Dillon.

"Barram dirra chen?" he shouted aloud. Lucy did not recognize these strange words.

"He's speaking in Samarran" said Barney looking down towards Lucy and Dillon, "We must be close to the forest. This is the language of the people of these parts of Astradan".

"Bernardo, the King's butler is from these parts, and speaks this language. He taught me a little. I'll try to say a greeting to this waykeeper" continued Barney.

Barney cleared his throat and was concentrating on what he was going to say in this language, which he didn't know too well.

"Kusana! Pira na tres amicas kingo barram" he finally announced.

Now, Barney had intended to say;

*"Hello! We are three friends of the King's"*

but he had mixed up his words in the Samarran language, and instead had said;

*"Chicken! We need three pineapples for the King".*

A frown formed on the troll's face and he placed his arms on his hips in annoyance.

"You call me a Chicken! How rude!" he barked.

Barney looked a little embarrassed; "I think I may have mixed up my words in Samarran" he whispered to Lucy.

"Huh! Your Samarran is very poor! Luckily, I speak your language too, traveller. Tell me what you want here – I assume it's not pineapples for the King?".

The frown had disappeared from the troll's face but he still held his arms to his waist, and stood directly in front of Lucy, Barney and Dillon, blocking their path over the bridge.

Lucy stood forward and offered a hand shake to the troll.

"Pleased to meet you Sir. My name is Lucy McTavish and these are my friends Barney Bracemaine and Dillon Batumi. Why, what a wonderful robe you have there sir".

The troll was actually dressed in an old brown robe, with holes and patches covering it from top to bottom.

A smile slowly started to form on the troll's face and he relaxed his arms, down to his sides.

"Well….. thank you madam, I had it specially made!". The troll looked delighted by the charming compliment that had been payed to him.

He pulled the sides of his scruffy robe outwards, in what almost looked like the sort of curtsy which a young girl would do in the presence of a Queen. This looked really funny and Lucy had to try hard not to laugh!

The troll now had a beaming smile upon his face.

"And I am Hasseus Hobb, waykeeper of the Eastern district of Ness Forest. Very pleased to meet you madam, and you're friends".

The troll gently shook Lucy's hand and gave a short bow to both Barney and Dillon.

"How can I be of assistance to you? What is a young girl like yourself doing this far away from the villages?" asked the troll.

"We are in search of a black crow which has stolen the Crystals of Astradan. It took them from the hand of Mowban the Wizard and flew in this direction" explained Lucy.

Next Barney joined the discussion; "If the crow takes the Crystals beyond the borders of Astradan, darkness will come to the kingdom and a deep freeze and never-ending darkness will set in. We must find the Crystals and we must find them soon".

The troll listened carefully, an expression of concentration filling his face. As soon as Barney finished speaking, the troll announced;

"Heard the jingling I did. This morning it was. I was asleep under the bridge, a very busy night I had you see, guarding the forest. I awoke to an unusual jingling sound. It sounded like a bunch of keys on a ring".

Lucy, Barney and Dillon listened carefully as the troll continued;

"I jumped up onto the bridge to see what this sound was but I could see nothing. Nothing at all around me! Then I realized the sound was coming from above my head!".

"Did you see the crow?" Dillon asked excitedly.

"Take a look at me and you may see the problem my friend; I don't possess a neck!".

Dillon felt embarrassed – sure enough, the troll's head seemed to run straight into his body. Without a neck, he was unable to look up to the sky.

"Oh, sorry sir, I didn't notice" said Dillon coyly.

"So I saw nothing but I know now – I am sure – that the jingling sound I heard was that of the Crystals you seek". The troll nodded knowingly as he spoke.

Barney looked beyond the bridge, over towards the beginning of Ness Forest, which could be seen about one mile in the distance.

"Then we must head into the forest, as planned" Barney said, looking towards Lucy and Dillon as he spoke.

"Beware, my friends. No-one has entered the forest for over two years" said the troll, "Since the rumours began".

"Rumours of what?" asked Lucy.

"Rumours that Kilmarvin, the Dark Knight, has made the inner forest his hiding place…. his home" answered the troll.

"But I thought Kilmarvin had left Astradan forever after he was defeated by Mowban?" questioned Dillon.

The troll sat back into his deck chair and spoke;

"Kilmarvin *did* leave Astradan, for the remote mountains of the Kingdom of Sirossa….. but rumour has it that he has returned to Astradan, although no-one would know why".

"Kilmarvin has come for his revenge against Mowban", suggested Barney in a worried voice.

"…..and I suspect the theft of the Crystals is connected with his quest for revenge" he added.

It was starting to feel a little colder now, although the early afternoon still provided plenty of pink-tinged daylight. Lucy zipped up the front of the coat that Miranda had given her.

"If you are going into the forest, you should go now" advised the troll. "It will become darker and colder soon. And if that crow passes beyond the borders of Astradan, it will become colder and darker still".

## 11

The forest blocked out a lot of the daylight, making it feel a lot later than it actually was. The thick trunks of fifty foot trees surrounded the three travellers, as they weaved themselves through the path.

The whistling of birds and chirping of small animals filled the air with sound. The forest was full of life.

"Do you have forests like this in your world, Lucy?" asked Dillon.

"Yes, there are Dillon" answered Lucy, "but I live far away from them. Where I live, there isn't much grass or trees or wildlife, just a lot of bricks and concrete!".

Dillon looked puzzled. "What is concrete, Lucy?".

"It's a hard, grey, dull material which homes are made from, where I live" replied Lucy. "It's not half as pretty as the natural things you use to make your homes, here in Astradan".

"Oh, I see" responded Dillon, trying to imagine the sort of world Lucy lived in.

"I'd love to see where you…...." just as Dillon was talking he suddenly shrieked out aloud and disappeared into a huge hole in the ground, that had been covered by thin branches and foliage.

"Arrrrrrrgh!".

Dillon disappeared into the hole completely, there was no longer any sign of him from where Lucy and Barney stood, shocked by what had happened.

At a super fast speed, Dillon flew down what looked like a huge slide, which ran from the surface of the forest, down, deep under ground.

It was like a combination between a steep, slide, and a wild, meandering rollercoaster.

"Whooooa!….. someone stop the ride!" shouted Dillon.

Lucy and Barney stood at the entrance to the hole, peering down into the seemingly endless darkness. They heard Dillon's call but could do nothing. After a few moments, there was silence.

"Dillon! Dillon! Are you ok down there? What happened?" Lucy shouted down the hole.

"He must be out of our reach now. The hole seems to have taken him far under ground!" Barney added.

"What should we do Barney?" asked Lucy, worried for her friend.

"I'm not sure. Perhaps I should jump into the hole after him, to see where he has gone?" suggested Barney.

Before Lucy could reply, however, a large wooden hatch started to swing upwards from the hole.

Within a couple of seconds it had completely blocked the hole. There was now no way in to where Dillon had gone.

"Oh no! What should we do now?" asked Lucy.

"This is not the trap of a wild creature or native of this forest, Lucy" started Barney. "This trap is too sophisticated. This is the work of Kilmarvin". Barney's voice sounded serious and concerned and Lucy shared Barney's worry.

# 12

After trying to open the wooden hatch without success, Lucy and Barney decided to continue into the forest. They had not forgotten their friend but they had to find a different way of getting Dillon back. It was unlikely that his way out would be back up through the hole. The slide that he fell down must have led somewhere.

"Perhaps I could help you".

The voice seemed to come from nowhere and startled Lucy. She reached out and held the cuff of Barney's sleeve.

"Who is it? Who's there?!" shouted Barney. The sky was becoming darker now – a deep purple haze replaced the pink glow of the daylight.

A small, square robot – the same type of robot as Wembot – slowly walked out from behind a tree to their left.

Whereas Wembot's steel casing was a silver colour, this robot had a dark black exterior.

It's metallic voice spoke once more;

"I can help you find your friend".

"How do you know we are looking for someone?" asked Barney, suspiciously.

"I saw what happened back there at the hole in the ground" replied the robot. "I have been following you since then, I wanted to get your attention but I did not want to startle you".

"Who are you?" asked Lucy.

"I am Zarbot. I belong to the guardian of this forest. I can take you to him, and he can take you to your friend".

"And who is this guardian of the forest?" asked Barney.

"His name is Mantagon ".

Barney turned to Lucy and whispered to her; "Mmm, there was a guardian of the forest called Mantagon. He was the cousin of King Boris. He did not enjoy life in the villages – so he came to live in Ness Forest."

Lucy glanced over at Zarbot and then back to Barney.

"So you think this robot seems to be telling the truth, and Mantagon could help us?" she asked.

"Well, the only strange thing is, Mantagon used to be in regular contact with the King. He would write and send messages via his horseman but a few months ago the King suddenly stopped hearing from Mantagon. The King and Queen became very worried about him" Barney explained.

"Didn't the King send someone into the forest to look for Mantagon? …..to check he was ok?".

"Well Lucy, when Mantagon left for the forest he asked that he be left alone, in isolation. This was his wish to the King before leaving. Some people in Astradan choose this sort of life, and their wishes are respected".

Lucy found it strange that a member of the village – the King's cousin at that – would want to go off into the forest to live alone. Wouldn't he be lonely? She wondered.

Zarbot spoke again; "We do not have long, daylight is fading".

"I think we have little choice Lucy. We should go with this robot and hope that it leads us to Dillon" Barney advised.

"I agree Barney, let's go".

# 13

They followed Zarbot through the meandering paths of Ness Forest. As the sky darkened, even the wildlife of the forest seemed to settle down for the night, causing an eery silence as they progressed into the heart of the vast woods.

At one point, a small hatch opened on the top of Zarbot's box-like body, and a small lamp extended out of his shell, lighting up the path for Lucy and Barney.

"How much further is it until we reach the Guardian?" Barney asked the robot that led their way.

"It is maybe two hours from here. If you wish, we can stop and shelter for the night?" suggested Zarbot.

"Do you want to stop Lucy?" asked Barney.

"I don't think we have time Barney. The crow may be close to leaving Astradan with the Crystals by now, or it may already have passed the borders" replied Lucy.

Barney knew Lucy was right. She may not understand everything about Astradan, and she may not fully understand exactly what would happen if the Crystals left the Kingdom, but she certainly knew how important it was to get them back to the safety of the village.

"Let's go on" ordered Barney.

# 14

After an hour or so, the forest became much thicker. Lucy and Barney could barely move forward because of all the foliage and bushes that now seemed to block the path. Zarbot cleared as much of the path as possible with his large, flat, steel feet but even he was finding it harder and harder to move through the dense forest.

"You must be very tired Lucy?" asked Barney.

"Yes I am a little tired Barney but we must find Dillon….."

Before Lucy could finish her sentence, there was a loud SPLASH!

Lucy and Barney peered through the small gap that Zarbot had cleared, ahead of them.

In front of them now was a huge lake! The forest had ended suddenly and the path ahead was now replaced by water.

## 15

In the distance, out into the centre of the lake, Lucy saw a small island, and on it, a tall black castle with jagged towers sticking out from it's main building, way up into the sky.

Shocked, Lucy looked over to Barney, then they both looked back across the lake to this magnificent but dark and eery castle.

"Please stand back" said Zarbot, who was now completely in the water, floating gently on the still surface of the lake.

As Lucy and Barney stood back a little, a large hatch opened on the top of Zarbot's square body.

After a few seconds there was a loud POP!

An orange blob shot out from the hatch on top of Zarbot, twenty feet into the sky, then landed on the surface of the water.

It started to unfold, and grew in size – within ten seconds, an orange, inflatable boat was floating on the lake, right next to Zarbot!

"Get into the boat please…" called Zarbot. "I will pull you along. I will take you to the Guardian of the Forest".

Barney went first. He stood on the edge on the bank and carefully hopped into the boat. He then held out his arm, took Lucy's hand and helped her as she carefully lowered herself into the boat.

Once aboard, they sat down, side by side in the middle of the boat – to make sure the craft stayed properly balanced.

Zarbot's main hatch closed and this time, a small circular door opened on the back of his steel shape. A long, thin cable came out. On the end of the cable, a small steel clamp attached itself to the front on the boat.

Using a small propeller built into his square, metal body, Zarbot started to pull the boat through the water, towards this mysterious island, ahead of them, in the middle of the lake.

# 16

As they drew closer to the island, Lucy looked up at the castle, which was a lot bigger than she had first thought.

"It doesn't look too friendly Lucy" suggested Barney, as the gentle swish sound of the boat moving across the lake filled the otherwise quiet evening air of the now dark night.

"Mmm, I know Barney" replied Lucy. "It doesn't look like the sort of place that Mantagon said he wanted to live, when he left the village".

"Yes you're right Lucy. Mantagon said he was moving to live in the forest itself. This dark castle doesn't look like somewhere Mantagon would call home".

As they reached the edge of the small island in the middle of the lake, Zarbot walked right out of the water and pulled the boat up onto dry land.

Lucy and Barney stepped out of the boat.

"Is this dark place the home of Mantagon, Guardian of the Forest?" Barney finally asked Zarbot.

"Come this way. We must go inside before darkness fills the night" said Zarbot, ignoring Barney's question.

The large hatch opened in Zarbot's body and the boat immediately deflated and was dragged back inside the robot, by the same steel cable and claw that had pulled the boat across the lake.

Zarbot set off towards a large, wooden, arched door at the front of the castle. Barney and Lucy followed close behind.

Suddenly, the wooden door opened with a loud creak, revealing nothing but darkness inside.

"Come" said Zarbot, as he started to walk through the door into the eery darkness inside.

"But it's very dark in there!" called Lucy.

"There will be light, once we are all inside" shouted Zarbot as he almost disappeared into the darkness inside the castle.

# 17

"Stay right by my side Lucy" said Barney, "We'll walk in together".

As they walked through the archway, the door behind them suddenly slammed shut.

They were now in complete darkness, unable to see anything.

"Barney!" shouted Lucy.

"I'm here Lucy, right next to you, don't worry" Barney reassured Lucy.

Just then, they heard two loud clashing sounds – it was the sort of noise you'd hear if two supermarket trolleys collided.

Then suddenly, it was as though a thousand light bulbs turned on!

Lucy and Barney immediately saw that they were both imprisoned in two separate cages that had been lowered from the roof on chains!

In front of them, Zarbot stood at the side of a large figure. A huge man wearing black armour, his face covered by some sort of helmet or mask.

Lucy looked around – they were in a large hall right at the front of the castle.

Hundred's of guards who wore red and black armoured uniforms stood around the edge of the hall, each holding a staff with a sharp V-shaped spear on the end. The hall had been lit up by four huge spotlights, that shone down from the arched roof.

"Master, here are the peasants that you ordered me to bring. They seek Mantagon. They seek also the boy" said Zarbot in his cold, mechanical voice.

Suddenly a roar filled the hall;

"Ha ha ha…..so, peasants of Astradan, you have come for your friend?".

The voice came from the tall figure ahead of them.

Lucy was scared but plucked up the courage to speak;

"We have come for our friend, Dillon. He fell into a secret passage in the forest and we couldn't get him back. Your robot brought us here to collect him sir" said Lucy nervously.

"I know all this, little girl!" roared the dark figure.

"Do you really think you are here by coincidence?!" he laughed.

The dark figure walked over to the two cages that held Lucy and Barney. He stood in front of Lucy's cage. He must had been at least twice her height.

"Do you know who I am, little girl?" he asked, almost whispering this time.

"*I* know who you are…." interrupted Barney from his cage, right next to Lucy's.

"…You are Kilmarvin….. Look, whatever problems you have with Mowban, there's no need to take it out on these children" continued Barney.

"I am The Dark Knight Kilmarvin!" screamed the dark, ominous figure. "The 6$^{th}$ Wizard of Astradan is of no concern to me!…..Soon he will be gone, frozen, along with all of Astradan!".

"Do you have the crystals?" asked Lucy.

Just then, they all looked to the roof of the large hall, as they heard a fluttering of wings. The black crow flew down from above and landed on Kilmarvin's shoulder – a black pouch in it's mouth – The Crystals of Astradan.

"Are you talking about these crystals?" asked Kilmarvin.

# 18

"Soon, these Crystals will cross the border and leave the Kingdom", continued the menacing figure. "….and when they do, Astradan will freeze over! The sky will fade. No man will be able to survive the ice age that will arrive when the Crystals leave the kingdom!"

Kilmarvin roared with laughter and snatched the pouch with the Crystals, from the mouth of the crow.

Then, suddenly, hatches in the floor beneath Lucy and Barney's cages opened and they both fell into the holes that had appeared. Beneath the holes were two long, steep slides. Lucy and Barney slid down the huge, long slides at what felt like the speed of sound!

After what seemed like minutes, Lucy suddenly landed on a huge stack of hay, Barney falling from a separate hole, and landing on the pile of hay, right next to her.

"My word, that was the fastest ride I've ever been on!" said Barney, catching his breath.

"Are you ok Lucy?".

"Yes, I'm fine" she answered, dusting the hay from her hair and clothes.

"Where are we?" she continued.

They seemed to be inside some sort of barn – the sort you'd find on a farm. However, there was no entrance or exit in sight. No sign of a door.

"This looks like some sort of stables" said Barney, looking around the barn at the piles of hay.

NEEEIIIIGHHHHHH !

They almost jumped out of their skin. Turning around, Barney and Lucy saw a beautiful, white horse standing behind them, tethered in the corner of the barn.

"What a beautiful horse!" said Lucy, walking over to the stunning creature and stroking the pure white mane of hair that stretched from the top of it's head to the bottom of it's neck.

"I think I know this horse!" said Barney.

"I believe this is Tirana, Mantagon's horse. This is the horse that he left the village on, in search of a peaceful life in the forest!".

Barney walked over to the horse. "Where is your master? Where in Mantagon, fine horse?".

As the horse heard the name of it's master, it raised up on it's hind legs, crying out.  NEIGHHHHH!

"I bet he wants to find his Master" said Barney.

"And we need to find Dillon…." Added Lucy, "…..and the Crystals".

Just then, a further voice was heard in the barn. A quiet, distant-sounding but clear voice.

"He doesn't seek his master – his master is here".

Lucy and Barney swung themselves around again but this time the could see no-one; not man nor beast.

"Who said that?!" called Barney.

"Who is it?" added Lucy.

"I'm up here, on the rafters" replied the mystery voice.

"It is my fault. All of your troubles are my fault" continued the voice.

Lucy looked up, above her head – perched on one of the rafters that held up the roof was a crow – the same crow that had stolen the Crystals.

"Look!" shouted Lucy, pointing up towards the crow.

"Is it you? …… that speaks to us?" asked Barney.

"Yes Barney, It is I, Mantagon" answered the crow.

"Mantagon?...... You're a crow?....what happened!?" Barney enquired, somewhat confused.

## 19

The crow flew down from the rafters and perched itself on the back of the fine horse, that they were all now sharing this barn with. The horse did not flinch.

"Mantagon, is it really you?" asked Barney once more.

"It is a sad story, Barney….. of greed and selfishness….." said the crow. "….and ultimately of betrayal".

"But you are neither selfish nor greedy Mantagon" replied Barney. "What took place to cause these strange events?".

"One summer evening, as I wandered Ness Forest in search of a new place to call home, I came ʋ a stranger. A strong, tall man. I was hungrʏ offered me food and water from his ˙ We sat and talked and told me he ʋ that he could perform magic" expla.

"He was good to me but he also seemed angry, bitter about something. He said he had once been a friend of the people of Astradan, of Mowban the Wizard but that he had been betrayed, so he left the villages for good".

"Why would the good people of Astradan betray this man?" asked Lucy.

"There was, in fact, no betrayal….." continued Mantagon.

"There was a flash of lightening so bright it almost blinded me, and then this man changed his appearance. Gone were his forest clothes and in their place was a dark suit of armour. This man was Kilmarvin. He suddenly cast a spell upon me!…." said Mantagon, becoming angry and upset.

"He turned my form into this dastardly crow!".

the betrayal was against you, Mantagon" ested Barney.

"There was more betrayal to come I'm afraid" explained Mantagon.

"Kilmarvin told me that he would only release me from the body of this crow, if I were to take the Crystals of Astradan and bring them to him".

Lucy stepped forward, closer to the crow. "You poor thing, you must have been desperately scared" she said. "But if Kilmarvin can cast those types of wicked spells, why didn't he go to Astradan himself and perform his evil magic on Mowban?".

"Because he is a coward" interrupted Barney. "Mowban could reverse this magic. In fact his spell is stronger than Kilmarvin's".

"Barney is right" said Mantagon. "I have only just won back my voice from the dark knight. He took it away, so that I would have no way of asking Mowban to release me from the spell!".

"So if you have given Kilmarvin the Crystals, why does he still hold you here, and why are you still in the form of a crow?" asked Lucy.

"Because, my dear, one should never trust an evil person", explained Mantagon. "He has given me back my voice but has imprisoned me in this barn with my horse, Tirana. He said he may still have use for me" continued the crow.

"Did you know what would happen to Astradan, should the Crystals leave the borders of the Kingdom?" asked Lucy.

"In my shame, I did" began Mantagon. "But I had no choice. Once I had given the Crystals to Kilmarvin, and he had taken away this spell, I was going to come straight to the village to get Mowban, so we could go after Kilmarvin together, and get back the Crystals".

"But Kilmarvin never kept his word, and he has left you as a crow?" suggested Lucy.

"That is right. I am a fool and I have betrayed the good people of Astradan, who will soon freeze in the pitch darkness" said Mantagon regretfully.

"You had no choice" said Lucy. "Don't feel bad. We will work this mess out".

Quite suddenly, Lucy realized that she was shivering. She felt very cold. She looked to her right and saw that Barney had started to shiver too, holding his hands around his elbows to keep the heat in his body. Even Mantagon, cursed to the form of a crow, now shivered, as did the beautiful white horse.

"It has begun" said Mantagon. "The Crystals have passed the borders of Astradan. This coldness is only the very beginning. Soon no man or animal will survive the freezing cold darkness that will come".

"Mantagon, who has the Crystals now?" asked Lucy anxiously.

"Kilmarvin knew I would not doom the people of Astradan by taking the Crystals beyond the border, so he gave them to his servant robot" he responded.

"So Zarbot now has the Crystals and he is taking them beyond Astradan?" asked Barney.

"He has already left the Kingdom – that is why the freeze has started. That is why there will be no daylight tomorrow morning" replied the crow.

"If only we could get out of this barn!" said Lucy.

"It is completely sealed" said Mantagon. "The wood that forms it's walls is twelve inches thick".

"That's no good then, we'd need a mechanical drill to get out from here" said Barney.

As they stood, wondering how they could possibly escape, Lucy, Barney and Mantagon all looked up to the high roof of the barn, beyond the rafters, as a quiet whirring noise became louder and louder. Sawdust began to fall from the roof into their faces.

Suddenly, a round piece of wood the size of a dustbin lid fell from the roof, crashing to the floor of the barn.

Lucy could see a small metal clamp on the end of a steel cable attach itself to the roof of the barn.

Then suddenly, a square, metal box jumped through the hole and started to lower itself down the steel wire.

"Wembot!" shouted Lucy.

Sure enough, the square metal object that had drilled a large hole in the roof of the barn - and which was now lowering itself to the floor - was Wembot.

"Hello Miss Lucy! I hope you don't mind that I'm here. It was wrong of me but I decided to follow you, Barney and Dillon into the forest, just in case you needed my help" said Wembot apologetically.

The robot landed perfectly on the floor of the barn and the metal clamp which had been attached to the roof released itself and shot back into Wembot's square box-like shape.

"We don't mind at all Wembot! You've saved the day!" said Lucy excitedly.

"Wembot, will you be able to track down Zarbot? Will you know where he has taken the Crystals?" asked Barney.

"The good news, Master Bracemaine, is that I can locate Zarbot because he has a microchip transmitter, and we can follow it's signal" said Wembot enthusiastically.

Everyone except Wembot was now shivering intensely.

"Is there some bad news?" asked Lucy.

"The bad news is that I have the same type of transmitter, so Zarbot may know we are coming". replied Wembot.

"I think we need some extra clothes" continued the robot.

Just then, the large hatch on his head opened up and two thick robes flew out, landing on the barn floor.

Lucy and Barney put on the robes and immediately felt a lot warmer.

"I'm afraid I have no clothes small enough for you in your current form, Mantagon…." said Wembot "….but you can fly with me if you like, it is warm inside my shell – all of my microchips and circuits generate a lot of heat!" said the robot.

"Thank you but I'll be fine. It may take our combined eyes to find and retrieve the Crystals, so I will fly alongside you" said Mantagon.

"Err….. did you say, *fly?*" asked Barney, somewhat nervously.

"Perhaps you and the girl should wait here – Wembot and I can go after the Crystals. It may be the only way we can catch up with Zarbot". suggested Mantagon.

"I'd like to come and help" said Lucy. "if it's possible".

"Anything is possible!" announced Wembot.
Small hatches opened in both of his sides and two small clasp-like steel hands protruded on two steel cable arms.

In what must have been thirty seconds, Wembot shot around the barn at lightening speed, picking up bits of scrap wood that were lying around. He then produced some strong rope from inside his steel shape and bounded the wood together.

In a miraculously short time, a rough but solid looking object that resembled a raft, sat in front of them all in the barn.

"Err, what is that?" asked Barney.

"It's your first class ticket on Wembot Airlines!" answered the robot, enthused.

"Can you carry us through the air on this thing Wembot?" asked Lucy.

"I can certainly carry one person! I'm not sure about two" came Wembot's response.

"There's only one problem….." added Mantagon. "How are you going to get it through that small hole is the roof?".

"Oh…." replied Wembot. "I, er, never thought of that!".

Lucy and Barney looked at each other and smiled.

Then, like lightening, Wembot disassembled the raft and shot up towards the roof with all the wood, disappearing through the hole.

In a matter of seconds he was back through the hole and landed safely on the floor of the barn.

"The aircraft is outside, fully ready!" he announced.

"Wow, you really work fast, don't you!" exclaimed Lucy.

"It's just as well. We must go quickly, we don't have much time" said Mantagon.

"Barney, there is only enough room on the raft for one person, and also, someone must stay here for Dillon" said Lucy. "Would you be willing to stay here?"

"I can't leave you to go alone" said Barney.

"I'll be safe with Wembot and Mantagon" said Lucy, reassuring Barney.

"What can I do to help, here?" asked Barney.

"Stay around here in case Dillon finds his way into the barn" replied Lucy.

"Come, we must go" said Mantagon.

The crow flew from his perch on the back of the horse, up to the roof of the barn and outside into the cold air.

Wembot gently took Lucy's hand. The steel clasp of his mechanical grip felt very cold against Lucy's skin.

Wembot slowly floated into the air, taking Lucy with him. They disappeared through the hole in the barn and landed on a grassy area near the outside of the barn. Lucy could see that the barn was at the rear of the castle, so hopefully they were out of sight from Kilmarvin and his guards.

Wembot lifted up the wooden contraption, which looked like a raft and placed it upon his square shape, holding it tightly in place with his metal hands.

"Hop on board Lucy, you'll be alright!" said Wembot, in his usual cheerful manner.

Lucy hopped aboard and held on tight. Wembot flew into the sky and Mantagon followed closely behind.

"Wow, I've never flown like this before!" shouted Lucy, as the wind blew through her hair.

They flew through the midnight sky. "This is the direction that Zarbot took" said Wembot.

"Ok….." replied Mantagon. "I'll keep my eyes on the ground below in case he has landed".

# 20

Barney sat on a pile of hay in the barn, close to Tirana, the white horse that belonged to Mantagon.

"If only there was a way I could find Dillon" he said out loud.

"I'd need to get out of this barn to do that" he continued.

"I don't know why I'm saying all of this to you", he now said to the horse. "It's not like I'm going to get a reply from a horse! ……. Then again, we have met a talking crow today!" he added.

"I wonder if there is any weak spot in this barn. A place where the wood is thinner".

Barney wondered whether he should have left the barn with the others. But leaving through the roof, simply took them outside of the castle. Barney needed to get out of the barn but back into the main building of the castle, in order to find Dillon.

He started to walk around the wooden walls of the inside of the barn, tapping the wood with his knuckles. The sound was quiet and high pitched – a sign that the wood was thick and solid.

As Barney reached the narrower back wall of the barn, close to where the white horse was tethered, he suddenly heard a much deeper, hollow sound.

"I found it!" he shouted. "I found a thinner section of the wooden walls!".

The sound of the thinner wood stretched from the ground, about six feet up the wall, where it then became thicker again. Barney had to stretch up on his tip toes to reach the point where the wood became thick again.

"This used to be a door" Barney said to himself. "It's been covered up by thinner wood, but there's probably a doorway, a passage behind this part of the barn!".

He tried to kick the wood but it was clearly too thick to break with his foot.

Then Barney had an idea.

"I need to get the horse to kick and break the wood!"

Barney called the horse by it's name and tried to tempt it away from it's current resting place – so that it could break free of the tether rope that kept it in this corner of the barn.

The horse did not move.

"Come on!" I need you to pull yourself free of this rope!" Barney now shouted at the horse.

But the horse did not budge!

Barney then stood right in front of the horse's nose, and shouted as loud as he could, flapping his arms up and down and jumping on the spot like a mad man!

Startled, the horse backed up briefly, then pounded forward, tearing free of the tether rope, knocking Barney into a nearby pile of hay.

Barney lay in the middle of the pile of hay, startled but uninjured. He glanced up and the horse was now free of the tether and was able to wander freely around the barn. "You done it!" said Barney to Tirana the horse, gently stroking it on the nose.

Tirana let out a joyful NEEEIGH !

# 21

Wembot, Lucy and Mantagon flew through the dark sky. It was getting colder and Lucy shivered. She wanted to rub her hands together to warm them up but needed both hands free to grab onto the wooden raft that sat upon Wembot's square body, as they flew through the air.

"Look ahead!" said Mantagon, who flew a few feet in front of Wembot and Lucy. "The border of the Kingdom".

Lucy could see below that the forest was ending and that directly ahead of them, lay a river. Beyond the river was a magnificent mountain range, running as far as the eye could see.

"Beyond that river, we are no longer in Astradan…" continued Mantagon, "….we are in the wild, mountainous Kingdom of Sirossa".

"What sort of place is Sirossa?" asked Lucy, having to shout so that Mantagon could hear her. "Will we be welcome there?".

"Sirossa is a huge, wild land. It's main towns and villages are far beyond this border and the mountains. There has been little contact between the people of Astradan and the people of Sirossa".

"Lucy, Mantagon, my sensors are picking up a signal from Zarbot. He is less than five miles from us!" said Wembot suddenly.

"Will he be able to pick up a signal from you Wembot? Will he know we are here?" asked Lucy.

"If he is awake. That is, unless he's in standby mode recharging his battery, in which case he will not be able to sense that we are close" replied the robot.

After flying for another minute or so, Wembot spoke again; "My sensors currently show that he is stationary. He doesn't seem to be moving at all, so he may be asleep in standby mode!" said Wembot excitedly.

"Then take us towards him" said Mantagon, "We don't have much time".

As they flew over the river and left the Kingdom of Astradan, they were quickly surrounded by the mountains.

"Has anyone noticed how much warmer it feels?" asked Lucy.

"That is because the Crytstals are here" said Mantagon. "So as Astradan starts to freeze and becomes uninhabitable, this part of Sirossa will warm up. But this is a mountainous area – people cannot live in these parts, so we must get the crystals back to Astradan".

## 22

They flew into the vast mountain range. It was a stunning sight; the mountains stretched as far as the eye could see. As the day started to break, a soft gentle pink daylight started to fill the sky ahead of them towards Sirossa.

Yet, when Lucy looked behind her, back towards Astradan, the sky remained as dark as it had been at midnight.

"Zarbot is less than one mile away, we must descend back towards the ground!" announced Wembot.

They gently drifted down towards a valley between the mountains. As they landed, Lucy removed the robe that Wembot had given her – she was warm now. The Crystals were lighting up the sky and generating warmth – but only here in Sirossa. She thought about how cold the villagers must be back in Astradan.

As Lucy stepped down from the makeshift raft, Wembot used his mechanical arms to remove it from on top of him and he placed it in a nearby bush.

"Come" said Wembot "Zarbot is this way". The Robot led the way, Lucy and Mantagon followed close behind.

After about fifteen minutes of walking, Lucy actually spotted Zarbot before Wembot had located his exact position.

"There he is!…." she whispered.

Wembot and Mantagon looked over in the direction Lucy had pointed and saw the dark, square shape of Zarbot, sitting in a small clearing, about fifty feet in front on them.

"We must approach very carefully…" said Wembot "…he will be in standby mode, but if we do anything other than whisper, his systems will come on line and he will awaken".

Lucy and Wembot tiptoed closer to Zarbot – Mantagon made no noise as he flew quietly through the air, close to the ground.

As they got within a few feet of Zarbot, Lucy pointed again, and whispered to the others in an excited voice;

"The Crystals!".

And there they were, still in the black pouch, but being tightly gripped in Zarbot's metal clamp of a hand.

"Should I try and pluck the Cystals from his hand?" asked Mantagon.

"Although he is currently in standby mode, charging his batteries, he still has great strength. We will probably need to use my mechanical cutters to free the pouch from his hand" replied Wembot.

"I have another idea" said Lucy.

"Wembot, do you have any scissors?" Lucy now asked still whispering.

The small hatch in Wembot opened up and this time, his cable-like left arm quietly protruded, with a set of large scissors attached to the end.

"Will these do?" asked Wembot "What are you planning Lucy?".

"It's simple! …… we just cut the pouch at the bottom and the Crystals will fall down into our hands!".

Lucy's plan was indeed an excellent one. Wembot and Mantagon had been thinking only of how they could pry open the mechanical hand of Zarbot, to get the pouch.

Lucy's simple but brilliant idea was to simply cut the pouch open and take the Crystals back.

# 23

Lucy stood not even two feet away from the dark, metal shape of Zarbot. She stayed absolutely silent and even ensured that her breathing was as quiet as possible.

Next to her, stood Wembot. His cable-like arm slowly approached Zarbot's identical arm, and the Crystals that were tightly held in his clasp-like hand.

As per the plan they had agreed moments earlier, Mantagon flew down next to Zarbot's short, thick legs. The Robot's legs were mechanical just like the rest of his body but at his knee joints, there was a small rubber cover on each leg, which prevented the wires and electronics of his knee joints from being exposed or damaged.

Mantagon began to peck and chew at the first rubber cover, quietly but quickly.

*Yuk, this tastes revolting!* He thought to himself.

As Mantagon pecked away, he thought about how soon, the spell that had turned him into a crow would be reversed by Mowban the wizard, and he would return to his human form. *But only if we can get these Crystals safely back to Astradan.*

While the crow chewed and pecked the rubber knee joints of the dark robot, Wembot's scissors now reached the bag and started to snip.

Soon, the scissors had cut a small hole in the bag and the first Crystal fell out of the bag and into Lucy's hand, which was carefully waiting below.

The crystal was a brilliantly illuminated blue colour – Lucy had not seen a colour like it before.

One by one, the Crystals fell from the hole in the pouch and into Lucy's hands. She placed each one into the safety of the inside pocket of her coat.

# 24

Back in the barn, Barney gathered all his strength and heaved his barrelled body up onto the horse. He stroked it's mane. "There, there…. that's it!" he said to the horse, hoping it wouldn't throw him down to the ground. Tirana the horse now seemed calm and did not object to having Barney on his back.

"Ok" started Barney "Now…we're going to jump over that haystack in the middle of the barn. So in order to get a good run at it, we need to go right into the corner over there".

Barney gently tugged the reigns and directed the horse towards the corner of the barn – the corner that had the thinner wood section, covering what used to be an entrance into the barn. *I hope this works* Barney thought to himself.

After a few minutes, Barney had cajoled the horse so that it was tucked tightly into the corner – it's bottom only a few inches from the blocked, hidden door.

"Now we need to jump that haystack, so you're going to have a take a really big run at it!" Barney said, hoping that somehow Tirana the horse would understand what he was explaining.

After a few moments, Barney sat up on the horse, his legs holding his entire weight into the stirrups, and shouted "GIDDY UP!!!…… LET'S GO!!".

The horse did not move.

"Come on!" shouted Barney.

Still, the horse stood.

"Do you want to help save your Master, Mantagon?…. Don't you want to help him reverse the evil spell that has turned him into a crooooooooow!".

Before Barney had even finished his sentence, Tirana jumped up on his back legs, let out an almighty kick, then charged at the haystack, clearing it with ease.

The horse landed on the other side of the haystack. Barney caught his breath then twisted his neck to look behind him –

The horse had done it!

There was a large hole in the corner of the barn, and behind it, a long corridor into the main building of the castle had been revealed.

"Well done Tirana!...." said Barney to the horse "I guess you really want to help Mantagon, don't you?".

The horse let out a short *neeeigh!* as if to agree with Barney.

"Well first of all, let's go and see if we can find Dillon, then we'll join Mantagon and the others" said Barney.

He led the horse through the large hole in the wall and up into the corridor that had appeared behind it.

It seemed to lead to a dark, underground part of the castle. An occasional candle attached to the stone walls provided at least some dim light.

As Barney rode the horse up the corridor, they turned a corner and Barney could hear something. It sounded like a small piece of metal bouncing repeatedly off the stone cold ground.

They proceeded slowly and quietly until finally, Barney saw straight ahead of them; a small dungeon cell.

Inside it, a small boy sat with his back to the bars, repeatedly tossing a coin into the air and watching as it fell to the ground.

"Dillon?" said Barney softly.

The boy turned around instantly – it was Dillon Batumi.

"Barney!" shouted Dillon excitedly "You found me!".

"Of course!" replied Barney "….I'm sorry it took some time but you'll be safe now".

"Now", continued Barney. "How are we going to get you out of this cell".

## 25

The last Crystal fell from the hole in pouch, into Lucy's hand. She placed it carefully into her coat pocket.

She looked up at Wembot as if to say *that's it, we have all the Crystals* but in fact, did not dare speak aloud, for fear of awaking Zarbot.

Mantagon had chewed through the rubber protective cover on one of Zarbot's knees and it was now clear to see what he had done – after chewing through the rubber cover, he had chewed through the electronic wires that passed from the short, stubby lower part of Zarbot's leg, to the upper leg joint which ran up and into his square body.

The crow now chewed furiously (but quietly) at the other leg.

Suddenly, in an instant, Zarbot's eyes lit up – a sign that he had come out of standby mode and was awakening.

He pulled up his arm – the one which now contained the empty black pouch – in front of his eyes, and let out a loud electronic gasp.
Zarbot swung the same arm straight into Wembot's body. It crashed into the other robot, as metal slammed against metal.

Wembot went flying into the air, landing upside down in a nearby bush.

Next Zarbot used his other arm and grabbed Lucy's arm tightly.

"Ouch! Let go! Let go will you!" she shouted but the dark robot held onto her tightly.

"GIVE ME THE CRYSTALS!" shouted the evil robot.

"Why don't you come over here and get them?" came the reply – from Mantagon, who hovered in the air a few feet in front of Zarbot.

"YOU HAVE THE CRYSTALS?" asked Zarbot.

"Yes I have swallowed them….." replied Mantagon "I am but a feeble bird, whereas you are a strong robot, so why not come and crush me and take back the Crystals?".

Just then, Zarbot released Lucy's arm and tried to charge at Mantagon.

But as he tried to move forward, both of his knee joints gave way and he crashed to the ground. He tried to stand and once again he toppled over, this time upside down.

"ERROR, ERROR!! Call technical assistance!" shouted the robot as it malfunctioned.

"Come on, let's get out of here!" called Mantagon.

With the Crystals tucked safely in her pocket, Lucy grabbed Wembot's hand. "Come on, there's no time to pick up the raft Wembot, you just fly and I'll hold onto your hand!".

"It could be scary Lucy" replied Wembot.

"I think this young Dreamscaper has proved her courage and bravery" suggested Mantagon.

As the three of them flew into the air and headed back towards Astradan, they could still hear the electronic moans and shouts from Zarbot, who was still trying to stand on his wobbling legs.

# 26

"I didn't think horses were strong enough to pull down iron bars" said Dillon, as Barney tied what had been left of Tirana's tether rope, around one of the iron bars that imprisoned the young boy.

"Well, normally they're not" agreed Barney "..but as I have found out, this is a pretty special horse, so we can only hope".

Once more, Barney mounted the stallion and prepared to launch the horse into a fast gallop.

"Ok, now Dillon, I just need to tell the horse to run by shouting ..........AAAAAAGHHHH!"

Again, before Barney could finish his sentence, the horse bolted forward, tearing the bar from the concrete that had held it in place.

"Wow, you did it!" shouted Dillon as he slipped out of the cell.

"Well, I can't really take the credit this time Dillon, I think Tirana knew what he needed to do!" replied Barney.

# 27

As they flew thought the air, Lucy, Wembot and Mantagon soon passed over the border, back into Astradan. The coldness hit them immediately.

"Lucy, we must stop, you need to put your robe back on!" suggested Wembot.

"No, we don't have time. I'll be ok. We must get back to the castle to rescue Barney and Dillon" Lucy replied.

Soon they reached the castle. From high in the sky they saw it on the horizon in front of them and after a few minutes, they were overhead the dark, eery place.

"Look!" shouted Lucy.

Down below, Barney and Dillon were on Tirana the horse, holding on tightly as the stunning creature was galloping at full speed away from the main castle building.

Behind them - giving chase - was Kilmarvin, who rode a jet black stallion, along with fifty of his guards, also on horse back and also giving chase.

Hovering from the sky above, Mantagon, closed his eyes and concentrated deeply.

*You can do it Tirana, you can do it.*

"Oh no, look!" cried Wembot this time. "They're approaching the edge of the island, there is nothing but water ahead of them!".

Tirana was indeed running out of land. The forest lay ahead of them but in between the safety of the forest, and the island that housed Kilmarvin's dark castle, lay much water.

*You can do it Tirana.*

As Mantagon opened his eyes, Tirana suddenly left the ground and flew into the air.

"Whooooooaaaaah!" cried Barney and Dillon as the horse climbed higher and higher into the dark sky.

"Arrrrrghhhhhhh!!….. go after them!!!" shrieked Kilmarvin but as his guards on horseback reached the edge of the water, they were thrown from their horses and landed in the water with a splash!

"You idiots!!!….." screamed Kilmarvin. "….I will show you how it is done!"

He ordered his horse towards the water at great speed. It kept galloping faster and faster.

Lucy was worried that Kilmarvin and his horse would also fly into the sky. "He's coming after us!" she called.

*No, he is not.* Mantagon thought.

Just then, from a great speed, Kilmarvin's horse reached the edge of the water and came to a sudden halt.

Kilmarvin was thrown twenty feet into the air and crashed into the water.

"Argggh…. You silly horse!" he screamed, while spluttering and spitting the dirty water of the lake from his mouth.

As Tirana joined the others in the dark sky, they all flew away from the island and the castle, and in the direction of the forest – and beyond it, the village.

As they flew along at high speed, Lucy glanced behind her and was amazed by what she saw.

As they travelled along with the dark freezing sky in front of them, the group left a trail of wonderful pink light and warmth behind them.

As the Crystals flew above Ness Forest, the light and the warmth was returning.

# 28

All of the villagers sat around the huge fire that had been lit on Tulip Green. The King and Queen sat shivering together, rubbing their hands to create a little more warmth.

"Poor things. How could I expect them to take on the evil of Kilmarvin?... I am such a fool" said Mowban the Wizard.

"It is not your fault" replied Queen Marrilla "We had to try to get the Crystals back. We had to try to save our village, and all of Astradan".

"They were so brave to go and try. Real heroes they are" said King Boris.

"We must honour them now, for I fear we do not have long left. We cannot survive this cold much longer" added the King. "Soon we must leave our homes and go in search of a new home, beyond Astradan".

Everyone on Tulip Green now stood around the large open fire, in absolute silence, thinking about their friends; brave Barney Bracemaine, young and courageous Dillon Batumi, and the Dreamscaper who had been first to volunteer to go after the Crystals; Lucy McTavish. The people of the village were not yet aware of the important and brave parts that Mantagon and Wembot had played.

"Friends and countryman, let us remember our friends who, so bravely, tried to save our kingdom from the evil forces...." started the King.

"We remember Lucy McTavish, the brave Dreamscaper. We remember Barney Bracemaine, much more than just a village baker. We remember....."

The king was suddenly and abruptly interrupted by Mowban the Wizard;

"Look, it's happening! The sky is falling in! Look at the bright lights falling from the sky!".

Mowban pointed up to the sky, where a bright light was tearing through the sky towards Tulip Green, a bright, colourful light, in it's wake.

"Wait a moment….." said the Queen "…Look! The light is returning to the sky!".

Sure enough, as the strange objects rocketed towards Tulip Green, the sky all around them started to light up with the familiar pink colour of the Astradan sky.

"Isn't that a flying horse?" asked Mowban.

"Isn't that the crow that stole the Crystals?!" asked the King.

"Isn't that Wembot?!" asked the Queen.

# 29

"They're back! Our heroes are back!…" screamed the King with wild excitement.

Tirana the horse softly touched down on the grass of Tulip Green, Barney Bracemaine and Dillon Batumi both on the stunning stallion's back. Shortly after, Wembot carefully lowered Lucy McTavish to the ground, before touching down himself. Finally, the crow, exhausted after flying for miles and miles through the dark and cold night, landed on Tirana's back.

The crowd cheered wildly, as the sky became brighter and brighter and the ice cold bite in the air gave way to a warm, pleasant temperature.

"But that is the crow who stole the Crystals, is it not!" shouted the King, once the cheers had finally subsided.

"No King Boris…." said Lucy in immediate reply "This is a true hero – this is Mantagon, the Guardian of the Forest".

The King, Queen, Mowban and pretty much eveyone else on the green looked startled; "Mantagon – is it really you?" asked the King.

"It is I, King Boris. I am so sorry for the trouble I have caused you and the people of the village" said Mantagon.

"Kilmarvin cast a spell and left me in this dastardly state – as a crow. However, it is this very state that has helped us to restore our Kingdom" added Mantagon.

Mowban walked across and stood directly in front of Tirana, the crow perched, almost lost in the vastness of the horse's back.

"You are brave Mantagon. You have always been a brave man, and even while cursed as a crow, you have been brave" said the Wizard.

"Lucy do you have the Crystals?" Mowban now asked.

Lucy pulled the bright, illuminating Crystals from the inside pocket of her coat and placed them carefully into the palm of Mowban's hand.

The Wizard smiled at her warmly. "You are a hero Lucy McTavish. Or a heroine I should say".

"I'm just happy I could help" said Lucy, beaming back at the white-coated wizard.

Mowban enclosed the Crystals in his cupped hands and held them up to the sky.

"Astora san morente a vivano!" shouted the Wizard.

Suddenly the light from the Crystals intensified greatly, huge jets of light streaming from the Wizard's hands into the bright pink sky.

Everyone on Tulip Green looked up towards the sky but then a sudden flash, as bright as lightening, brought the attention of the people back down to the ground.

A hundred gasps were heard;

Where moments earlier, the small, black crow had sat upon the back of the stunning stallion Tirana, now the crow was gone.

In it's place, seated upon the horse, was a tall knight, wearing silver armour so bright you could see your reflection in it.

The knight removed his helmet, and beneath it was a strong, handsome face, with locks of dark hair flowing to his shoulders.

This, was Mantagon, Guardian of the Forest.

The crowd roared and cheered. Mantagon rode Tirana for a lap of honour around the green. They approached the King's chariot at great speed as everyone held their breath, expecting a collision but at the last moment, the horse leapt ten feet into the air and landed safely on the other side of the King's transport.

The crowd cheered and clapped ecstaticly.

"People of Astradan….." started the silver knight "….from this moment on, I am no longer the Guardian of the Forest".

The people of the village looked at one another, in anticipiation.

"I am now the Guardian of Astradan!" announced Mantagon "I will protect Astradan, it's people, and the Crystals from future evils!".

The crowd erupted into a deafening roar.

Mowban picked up Lucy McTavish and placed her on his shoulders.

"Three cheers for the heroine of Astradan!" shouted the Wizard.

HIP HIP, HOORAY !!
HIP HIP, HOORAY !!
HIP HIP …………

Suddenly, Miranda Moon looked up at Lucy and gave her a kind, caring smile.

"Lucy, you're going to be late. They'll be here soon" said Miranda.

"Who?… who will be here".

Suddenly, Lucy noticed the light fading and the excitement and exhaustion of the last twenty four hours, and her adventures in Astradan, seemed to catch up with her.

## 30

"Lucy, come on, didn't you hear me….. they'll be here soon".

Lucy rubbed her eyes for a few moments, "Who'll be here soon? She asked", finally opening her eyes.

"Sally and Zara. Sally's Dad is taking the three of you bowling remember!" said Lucy's Mum.

Lucy jumped up with a start, and looked around the room. She recognized this room – it was not Miranda Moon's guest room, it was Lucy's bedroom at home.

"Goodness gracious Lucy, you look like you've been to the moon and back!" said Lucy's Mum. "Well, welcome back home sweetheart"", Lucy's Mum gave her daughter a big hug.

"Now come on sleepy head, time to get up, you've got an exciting morning of bowling ahead of you!".

## 31

"Hey Lucy!" said Sally, as Lucy walked down the path at the front of her home, towards Sally's Dad's car.

"Hi Bezzie, how are you?" said Lucy, giving her friend a hug.

"Cool! You jump in the back of the car with Zara, I'm in the front with my Dad" said Sally excitedly.

Lucy jumped in the back of the car and gave her other best friend a hug. "You look shattered Luce!" said Zara.

"Um, yes, I didn't get much sleep last night" said Lucy, smiling to herself.

## 32

As the girls put on their bowling shoes, they got ready to play.

"Oh look who's here" said Sally, pointing to the next bowling lane.

It was Michaela, Jade, Carly and Caitlin.

"Well, look who it is….." said Michaela in her usual cat-like tone. "The girls who *weren't* at the party of the year last night".

"Oh sorry I couldn't make it, I had something really important to do – I had to mop the kitchen floor" said Sally sarcastically. Zara and Lucy giggled with laughter.

"Huh!" grunted Michaela "I bet none of you had as exciting a night as we had!".

Lucy smiled to herself, and prepared to score her first strike of the morning.

*I wouldn't be too sure about that!* she thought to herself.

## ~ THE END ~

*Lucy will return in:*

**The Plague of Astradan**

*~ A Lucy McTavish Adventure ~*

*Contact:*

Email: misterdavidrogers@googlemail.com

Tel:     (07950) 350 840

Website (coming soon):

www.davidrogers-author.co.uk

Other books, coming soon in the Lucy McTavish series:-

*The Crystals of Astradan*
*The Plague of Astrandan*
*Christmas in Astradan*
*Journey to Sirossa*